Genie
Meanie

Genie Meanie

Mahtab Narsimhan

illustrated by
Michelle Simpson

orcaEchoes

ORCA BOOK PUBLISHERS

Published in Canada and the United States in 2021 by Orca Book Publishers.
orcabook.com

Library and Archives Canada Cataloguing in Publication
Title: Genie meanie / Mahtab Narsimhan ; illustrated by Michelle Simpson.
Names: Narsimhan, Mahtab, author. | Simpson, Michelle (Illustrator), illustrator.
Series: Orca echoes.
Description: Series statement: Orca echoes
Identifiers: Canadiana (print) 20200182250 | Canadiana (ebook) 20200182285 |
ISBN 9781459823983 (softcover) | ISBN 9781459823990 (PDF) | ISBN 9781459824003 (EPUB)
Classification: LCC PS8627.A77 G46 2021 | DDC jc813/.6—dc23

Library of Congress Control Number: 2020931805

Summary: In this partially illustrated chapter book, an eight-year-old
girl confronts a bully with the help of a genie she discovers has
been living in a spice bottle her grandmother left her.

Orca Book Publishers is committed to reducing the consumption of
nonrenewable resources in the making of our books. We make every
effort to use materials that support a sustainable future.

Orca Book Publishers gratefully acknowledges the support for its publishing
programs provided by the following agencies: the Government of Canada,
the Canada Council for the Arts and the Province of British Columbia through
the BC Arts Council and the Book Publishing Tax Credit.

Cover artwork and interior illustrations by Michelle Simpson
Author photo by Dean Macdonnell of Macdonnell Photography
Edited by Liz Kemp

Printed and bound in Canada.

24 23 22 21 • 1 2 3 4

For Rahul and Aftab.

Chapter One

I missed Gran so much, it was like having a stomachache that wouldn't quit. No one could fill the hole in my heart that she'd left when she died. Not Grandpa, who was visiting from India, and not my parents or my best friend, Bai Leng. Grandpa had brought a box of treasures Gran wanted me to have, but this made me miss her even more.

Gran was the only one who'd understood that school was tough. Kids could be super mean. She'd encouraged me to stand up for myself if anyone tried to bully me. *Never give up trying to do the right thing, no matter how hard it is*, she would say. *But try not to hurt anyone either*. How was I going to face another year of school without her?

I frowned at the odds and ends I'd tipped out of the box onto my bed. Why had Gran left these things for me? A crow's feather, a yellow pencil stub, a necklace made of wrinkled brown beads, a rusty key and a small glass bottle with some kind of spice in it. I searched for a note. Nothing.

What was I going to do with the spice? Mom didn't let me use the stove— Gran had known that. All of this stuff was junk—wait a minute. I stared at the bottle. It was labeled *Zayn Garam Masala*. A wisp of blue smoke seemed to waft up and down inside it, and I had the weirdest feeling it was trying to escape.

I rattled the bottle.

Oi! Stop!

Startled, I looked around. "Who said that?" My desk and chair returned my gaze mutely.

"Kiara!" Mom called from downstairs. "Dinner's ready!"

I was dying to examine the bottle more closely, but Mom liked everyone at the dinner table on time. I scooped up Gran's things and put them back into the box. Except the bottle of garam masala. I picked it up. "Ouch!" It was so hot, I dropped it. "Oh no!" Luckily it landed on the carpet with a thud.

Watch it, butterfingers!

"What? Who? Come out and show yourself!" I said, inching toward the door. Bai had texted to let me know he was back from his vacation in China and had precisely one day to get ready for school. I needed to ask if he knew anything about ghosts, because either my room was haunted or I was losing it, but I'd have to wait until tomorrow.

No one appeared. *I* was the only kid in this house. But the voice I was hearing in my head also belonged to a kid. It kind of sounded like this horrible boy in my class, Matt.

I gazed at my reflection in the mirror. Brown eyes stared back at me from under a mass of wriggly black hair. "Kiara, you're only eight and you're losing your mind," I said to myself. "That's sad!"

Yup! the voice in my head agreed.

I picked up the bottle, which was barely warm now, and put it on the desk. *This was so weird.*

"Kiara Prasad, I want you at the dinner table, now!" Mom's voice had a sharp edge.

I glanced at the bottle once more before I left the room.

The smoke inside was now blood red.

Chapter Two

I raced through dinner even though it was my favorite, shrimp curry and rice. Normally I would enjoy each bite and take a second helping. But today I had Zayn Garam Masala on my mind. I couldn't wait to get back to my room.

"First day of school tomorrow, Kiara," said Grandpa. "Ready for third grade?"

No! If Gran were here, I would have confided to her that I was scared.

Although most of my classmates were okay, Matt the bully loved to pick on Bai and me. The thought of facing him again made my stomach clench. The curry and rice wanted to climb right back out. But I wasn't announcing this at the table. Mom would tell me it was only first-day jitters, that things would get better once I settled down. With Matt, things only ever got worse.

I shrugged. "Sort of."

Grandpa stroked my hair. "You'll be fine."

I nodded. "May I be excused, please? I have to get ready for tomorrow."

Mom nodded. Grandpa gave me a sad smile. "Leela would be so proud of her granddaughter starting third grade. She would have made your favorite coconut burfi to celebrate."

I hugged him before I left the table. He was missing Gran just as much as I was. Maybe a tiny bit more.

I raced into my room. The bottle was exactly where I'd left it. A wisp of smoke, blue again, floated to the top and then back down, over and over. I picked it up and sat on the bed. The glass was cool under my fingertips. Earlier it had been hot, then warm. What was going on? Was this a magic-trick bottle from Gran's childhood days? How did it work? What did it do?

What are you waiting for? Diwali? Open it.

This time I didn't bother looking around. The bossy voice was in my head. And I didn't like it. At all.

I ran a finger around the screw-top lid. Did I dare?

Hurry up!

"Hope I'm doing the right thing, Gran," I whispered to myself as I started to unscrew the lid. It was rusty and didn't budge. I tried harder. My fingers kept slipping.

Put some muscle into it!

"Shut up!" I said.

"That was rude, Kiara," said Mom, who happened to be passing by my room. "Who're you talking to?"

She popped her head in just as I shoved the bottle under my pillow and grabbed a book. "No one. I was reading aloud."

"Hmm." Mom didn't look entirely convinced. "If your schoolbag is packed, I suggest you go to bed. Good night."

"Good night!" I said.

Mom shut the door gently. I picked up the bottle again. Red smoke zoomed inside like a mini tornado.

I took a deep breath and put all my strength into unscrewing the top. After the first couple of turns, it was easy. As soon as the lid popped off, the smoke shot out and straight into my eyes, blinding me. It felt like someone had thrown a handful of pepper into my face. The stink of stale spice filled the room.

"It's been a thousand years since my last shower!" someone said in a disgusted voice. "GROSS!"

I scrubbed my watering eyes and opened them. A boy dressed like an Indian maharaja stood at the foot of my bed. He wore tight white pants scrunched up at the ankles and a red-gold tunic that ended below his knees. Spiky black

hair stuck out from under a red turban. His emerald-green eyes stared into mine as he took off his turban and gave a deep bow. "Thank you for releasing me, Scrawny Human," he said with a cool smile. "At your service...*not*!"

I backed up against the wall. "Are you—"

"Yes," he said. "I'm Zayn, a genie. And I desperately need a shower. Show me the bathroom and go get me some food. I'm *starving*!"

Chapter Three

I stared. And stared. A minute passed, then two. Zayn walked around the room, examining everything, smirking at me now and then.

"You're a real, live *genie*?" I asked.

"Yes and yes."

"The magical kind?" I said.

"Bingo!"

"One that can grant *three* wishes?" I said, fingers crossed behind my back.

"Oui, madame!" he said. "And make that unlimited wishes. *Three* is so last millennium."

"As many as I like?" I asked, just so there was no confusion. I was already making a mental list of all the things I wanted.

"Si, señorita!" he said.

"Someone who will do my every bidding!" I said. "Like in the Aladdin story?"

"Whoa!" said Zayn, tossing his stinky turban onto my bed. "We'll have to discuss that. But before we do anything, I need a shower and something to eat."

I stared at him. "My name is Kiara, and you've forgotten the magic word."

He raised an eyebrow. "We don't use magic words these days. Too old-fashioned."

"I meant *please*," I said. "And *thank you*. *Sorry* too, if you've done something wrong."

Zayn stopped in mid eye roll when I glared at him. "*Please* get me something to eat or you'll be very *sorry*," he said with a charming smile. "*Thank you*."

He did smell like an overcooked curry and badly needed a shower. "I'll get you a snack. The bathroom is right there."

Gran had never told me *anything* about a genie. How did she get him? Was Zayn real or had the stress of facing Matt tomorrow made me lose my mind already? I stared at the empty bottle. The label explained his name, *Zayn* Garam Masala. I'd make him explain everything else to me later.

Mom was cleaning up in the kitchen.

"May I have a snack before bed?" I asked.

She looked surprised but agreed. "Would you like an apple with peanut butter?"

"How about some more of your delicious curry and rice *plus* the apple with peanut butter?"

"I thought you'd eaten your fill at dinner, but all right," said Mom with a laugh. "Once you finish, bring the dirty dishes down and put them in the dishwasher, please."

I carried the food upstairs on a tray, shut my door and piled some books and stuffies against it. Early warning system in case Mom decided to drop in while I was negotiating my wish list with Zayn.

Minutes later he walked out of the bathroom, wearing a pair of shorts and my favorite yellow T-shirt and smelling of my watermelon shampoo. A whiff of garam masala still clung to him. It would probably take another thousand years of scrubbing to get rid of *that* smell.

"Hey!" I said. "Who said you could wear my clothes?"

"My clothes stank. And these are so soft and comfortable," he said.

"Eat, and then we talk," I said, pushing the tray toward him. "I'll give you my wish list. The first thing I want is for you to take care of the bully, Matt."

Zayn sat cross-legged on the carpet and inhaled the food, pausing only to say, "Your mother is a great cook!" Within seconds the plates were wiped clean. He burped loudly.

"Manners!" I said.

Zayn burped even louder. "You may ask your questions now, Kiara."

"How did you get into that bottle?"

Zayn shook his head. "Long story, and I'm too tired to tell you now. Next?"

"Can everyone see you, or am I the only one?"

Before he could answer, there was a knock on my door. I jumped up so quickly I almost fell over. How would

I explain why I had another kid in my room without permission? Mom was going to have a cow.

"May we come in, Kiara?" Mom called. "Grandpa wants to say good night."

"Hide!" I said to Zayn as I pushed the books and stuffies out of the way and opened the door. But he just lounged on the carpet and yawned.

I was going to be deader than the mutton leg defrosting in the fridge. Mom stood outside my room with Grandpa.

"Good luck tomorrow," Grandpa said, kissing my forehead. "And good night."

"Night, Grandpa," I replied. "Thank you."

Mom glanced at the empty tray and walked into my room to get it. I expected her to yell any second now. Zayn sat inches from her feet, grinning.

"You must have been hungry," said Mom. "Make sure you eat a proper meal tomorrow. Now it's time for bed. I'll take these downstairs."

I shut the door and stared at Zayn. "Only I can see you?"

"Jawohl," said Zayn, with a yawn so wide his jaw cracked.

"Can I tell my best friend, Bai, about you? He would *love* to meet you. He's really into Chinese mythology, ghost stories and all things magic."

"You can tell no one! You want wishes granted, and I want privacy. If you told your friend, he would want wishes too. No. Can. Do. I only ignore—I mean, *listen* to one master at a time."

"Okay, okay!" I said. "Let's talk about my wishes."

Zayn yawned again. "I've been standing up forever. It'll be nice to lie down." He snapped his fingers. A small four-poster bed with a purple canopy appeared by the window. It had matching silken covers and piles of squishy pillows. He raised his arms over his head like a professional swimmer and dived in.

"You can't sleep yet!" I said. "I haven't told you what I want."

"How about you tell me in a thousand years," he said, closing his eyes. "I'm on vacation. Starting now."

"But—but I'm your master...err, mistress? Either way you *must* do my bidding!"

Zayn gave an extra-loud snore.

Chapter Four

Zayn was still sleeping when I left for my first day of third grade the next morning. I poked his foot. Rock solid. I had not been imagining things, nor was I losing my mind. This evening I would show him who was boss! What was the point of a genie (with unlimited wishes!) if you couldn't get him to do your bidding?

"Hey, Kira-Kira, welcome back!" said Matt the moment I entered class. "We're going to have a fun year, weirdo!"

I kept a straight face though my heart was pounding. I remembered the time he'd pushed my swing so hard that I'd fallen off and scraped my hands and knees. There were many more incidents than that, but this one had been the scariest. I ignored Matt, found a seat by the window and saved one beside me for Bai.

"Kiara!" an excited voice called out.

"Bai!" My best friend charged into the classroom. He was tanned, with straight black hair that fell to his shoulders. Today it was tied back in a ponytail. As always he wore horn-rimmed glasses, khakis and a white shirt. I had tried to get him to wear a hoodie once in a while to tone down his too-neat look, but he'd refused, and I respected that.

"And here comes weirdo number two," said Matt from his seat across the room.

"Leave us alone," I said, trying to sound firm.

"I second that!" said Bai.

Matt laughed, and his buddies joined in.

"Good summer holidays?" Bai said, plunking down on the seat beside me.

"My gran died. I miss her a lot." My voice wobbled, and I looked out the window, trying not to bawl so Matt wouldn't have more to tease me about.

Bai gave me a big hug. "Sorry I wasn't here for you. My parents had a lot of stuff to take care of, and we stayed in China longer than we'd planned. We only came back a day ago, or you and I could have hung out before school."

"At least you came back! I don't have to face third grade on my own." We both glanced at Matt.

"This year is going to be better," said Bai. "Because we're not going to let him bully us. We'll fight back. Right?"

"Right!" I said. I knew I had Zayn, and the first wish he was granting me was to stop Matt from picking on us.

"I got you something," said Bai, digging into his bag. He gave me a notebook with a brilliant red dragon, breathing fire, on its crinkly cover.

"This is beautiful," I said, flipping it open. Blank, smooth pages waiting to be filled. I turned it over. Made in China. I grinned. "Thank you."

"You're welcome," said Bai, smiling back. "Nothing like that in India, right?"

"Ha—*better*!" I replied.

We had a running competition about things made in India versus in China. We both tried hard to convince the other that our own country's products were superior. Neither of us budged an inch.

"Kira-Kira and Bye-Bye sitting on a desk," Matt sang. "Making a big mess, mess, mess."

My face turned hot as some of our classmates started giggling.

"SHUT UP or you'll be sorry!" I yelled, banging my fist on the desk.

School had not even begun, and he was already teasing us.

Our teacher walked in just then. He was tall, with glasses and thinning hair. He seemed to fill up the room as he frowned at me. "I don't tolerate this kind of behavior in my class. Please apologize to your classmate."

This was so unfair! I apologized to Matt through gritted teeth. His mean smile made me even angrier.

"It's all right, Kiara," Matt said. "I forgive you."

"All right, settle down, everyone," the teacher said in a booming voice. "My name is Mr. Walters. Welcome to third grade."

"I'll show him this year," I muttered to Bai, a volcano bubbling in my chest. "I have a plan."

"What plan?" said Bai.

"Um…er," I stammered. I'd forgotten I wasn't supposed to tell *anyone* about Zayn. "Tell you after school," I whispered, buying time.

"You two," said Mr. Walters, pointing at us. "No talking, or I'll have you sit separately."

"Sorry," we said in unison.

Mr. Walters took attendance, then told us to share one interesting thing about ourselves. "I'll go first," he said. "I love history and ancient civilizations. No matter where I go on vacation, my first stop is always a museum."

"I can fold my tongue in half," said Tara. And she demonstrated for us. Immediately the rest of the class tried it, but no one could do it as well as she could.

"I collect insects," said Abdi. "The creepier, the better."

"I love to travel," said Bai. "But my home country, China, is my favorite place to go." He looked at me.

"I love watching Hindi movies," I said when it was my turn. "I'm going to be an actress when I grow up. And India is the best place in the whole wide world." I glanced at Bai, who shook his head slightly.

Matt laughed out loud, and his buddies joined in. "You two are so funny."

"Nothing funny about appreciating where you came from," said Mr. Walters. "Do you know the population of your countries?" He looked at Bai and me.

"One-point-four billion," said Bai promptly.

"One-point-three-six billion," I said just as promptly.

"Well done," said Mr. Walters. "I wouldn't be surprised if India caught up to China in the next decade. Both countries seem to have a healthy competition going on."

Just like Bai and me. I smiled at my friend, and he smiled back.

"Thank you, class, for sharing. It's given me a better understanding of all of you. Now let's fill those heads with information, shall we? Take out your notebooks, please."

I wondered what Zayn was doing and if he'd be ready to grant me my wishes when I got home.

Chapter Five

We sat at a corner table in the cafeteria during recess. Normally we went to our special spot on the playground, a hollow in the trunk of a large maple tree. The leaves were so dense that even if it rained, we didn't get a drop on us— that is, until the leaves fell off in the fall. But today Bai wanted to check out the library after lunch, so we stayed inside.

I'd brought a grilled chicken sandwich with carrots and hummus. Bai dug into a beef-and-rice bowl, which was still steaming. He asked me to try a bite. It was delicious. "How does it stay so hot? Your mom must have packed it hours ago."

"Thermos was made in China," said Bai through a mouthful of food. "Much better than your Indian tiffin."

"You wish!" I said, crunching a carrot. "The tiffin has four compartments. Yours has only one."

We bumped fists, smiling.

"So what's the plan to deal with Matt?" Bai asked.

Before I could reply, Matt appeared at our table. I froze. Bai swallowed his mouthful and almost choked. Matt thumped his back—hard. Bai glared at him.

"Hand over some money, you two," he said. "I forgot mine, and I'm hungry."

Just like that, it had started again. If we didn't do something, this year would be the same as the last. But do *what*? Zayn wasn't here. I glanced around quickly. The teacher was too far away, chatting with the lunch server. Matt seemed to have excellent timing, or he was smart enough to approach us when he knew no one was watching.

"Leave us alone, Matt," said Bai, his voice shaking. "Or I'll tell the teacher *and* the principal about your bullying. And anyway, we don't have any money."

"Do it, then," said Matt, sneering at Bai. "Go on. Call the teacher!" He sat down. Two other students at our table picked up their lunches and hurried away. I didn't blame them.

Bai stood up and waved, trying to attract the teacher's attention. My heart zoomed into my mouth. "Bai, don't!" I said, but he ignored me.

Matt swept Bai's thermos off the table. It cracked, and the food splattered on the floor. Bai stared at Matt, then at his spilled food.

"Oops, clumsy me," said Matt, standing up. "This isn't over, you two," he said as he strolled away.

I sat on the bench like an ice sculpture, hating myself for not being able to stand up to Matt or help Bai. If Zayn had been here, we could have taught Matt a lesson.

"You could have yelled for the teacher too," said Bai. "Matt wouldn't have been able to stop us both."

"I told you not to try anything," I said.

"We have to stop being cowards and stand up to him," he said, his eyes flashing. "Isn't that what we decided, or have you changed your mind?"

"You can share my lunch," I said, though his words stung like a wasp's bite.

He shook his head and walked away.

I found that I'd lost my appetite too.

Bai didn't talk to me for the rest of the day. As soon as the bell rang, he swept his things into his bag and hurried out of the classroom. I raced to catch up with him in the hall. I prayed Matt would leave us alone. Things were bad enough already.

"Bai, wait up!"

He stopped.

"I'm sorry I didn't help," I said. "You know what Matt's like."

"I know, and that's why we have to *do* something this year," said Bai, taking our usual route through the park. "We can't do nothing! I'm tired of being scared of that bully."

"Matt could hurt us," I said, walking faster than Bai now.

"Not if we stick together and fight back," said Bai. "Hey, what's your hurry? Someone waiting for you at home?"

"Nope, he's right here," said a voice I recognized. "How do I look?"

And there was Zayn, prancing alongside us, grinning. He'd found my stash of old Halloween costumes and was dressed as a pink unicorn. I suppressed a desperate urge to giggle. I said nothing, knowing it would look weird if I talked to thin air.

"My grandfather is waiting," I said to Bai. "He's visiting from India and likes to spend as much time with me as possible."

"Sweet. May I come over and meet him?"

"Sure!" I said, happy that Bai wasn't mad at me anymore. We cut across the soccer pitch.

"Is that your best friend?" Zayn asked. "Ask him if he'll lend me his outfit. It's so cool."

"Shut up," I whispered.

"I didn't say anything," said Bai, looking confused.

"Sorry, just talking to myself," I said.

Over Zayn's laughter I heard thundering footsteps behind me.

"Run, Bai!" I said, looking back. "It's Matt."

"Stop him, Zayn," I said under my breath as I pumped my arms and legs. "Trip him or something."

I'd run a short distance before I realized Bai wasn't beside me. I stopped and looked back. Matt was emptying Bai's satchel onto the grass. He'd picked a spot where no one else was walking by and the trees shielded them from the pedestrian path.

"Zayn, do something," I said. But he just leaned against a tree trunk, watching Matt and Bai arguing. "Please! I *command* you to do my bidding!"

"If you're so worried about your friend, *you* do something," Zayn said. "I'm on vacation, remember?"

"I know you have money, Bai," Matt growled. "Give it to me."

"Kiara, HELP!" Bai shouted.

Once again I froze, my heart pounding against my ribs.

Matt raised a foot and slammed it down on Bai's pencil case. There was a crunching sound.

"No!" yelped Bai.

"Last chance," said Matt. "Don't make me hurt you."

Bai's hand shook as he got his extra lunch money out of his pocket. His face was as white as his shirt.

"Wow, I'm rich!" said Matt, snatching the bills from Bai. He waved to me. "You're next, Kira-Kira!"

To my horror, my feet turned and ran, taking me along with them.

Chapter Six

"How could you stand by and watch my friend being bullied!" I yelled at Zayn. "You could have done something, you useless genie!"

"Why didn't *you* do something?" asked Zayn, taking off the unicorn costume.

I flopped on the bed and stared at the ceiling. The scene replayed in my mind like a movie on repeat. I was such a loser. I hadn't helped my friend. I'd run away.

I'd. Run. Away.

Dinner tasted like pencil shavings.

"Why aren't you eating, Kiara?" Mom asked.

"Not hungry, Mom."

"Tough day at school?" asked Grandpa, stroking my hair.

You have no idea. I would have given anything for a clove-scented hug from Gran. I swallowed the lump in my throat.

"You'll settle down in a day or two," said Dad, cutting up a piece of grilled mutton.

Zayn hovered beside the table, pointing to the food and rubbing his belly. I ignored him, just like he'd ignored my pleas earlier that day. It was hard to focus on everyone's questions and keep an eye on Zayn at the same time. His hand hovered over the garlic bread.

If he picked it up, would everyone see it floating in midair, or would it just disappear? How would they react? I was in no mood to find out.

"No!" I said, glaring at Zayn.

"No need to yell," said Mom, continuing a conversation I hadn't heard.

"We won't go to the new Hindi movie on the weekend if you feel that strongly about it. I thought it would cheer you up."

I shot Zayn a dirty look. He'd timed this perfectly. I'd yelled at the precise moment Mom was asking about the movie I'd been wanting to see. He was more trouble than help.

"Um, I have some reading homework," I said. "May I eat dinner in my room, please?"

"I prefer that you eat with us," said Mom. "But I'll make an exception just for today. You may go."

I piled my plate with more garlic bread, grilled meat, green salad and a piece of blueberry pie. It would be mean to starve Zayn, even if he hadn't helped out today. He did a happy dance around the table as he eyed the food.

Back in my room, Zayn balanced the plate on his knees and tucked in to the meal.

"If you can do magic, why can't you conjure a meal for yourself?" I asked.

"Magicked food tastes horrible," he said. "Now shhh. Let me eat."

I wondered what Bai was doing. He was so mad at me for running away. I would be mad at me too. How was I ever going to make it up to him?

I sent him a text saying I was sorry. There was no reply.

Zayn finished eating and wiped his face with the back of his hand. "So good *and* there was no garam masala in it!" he said and burped. "Can't stand the smell of that spice."

"Your turn to help me," I said.

"You have the pleasure of my awesome company," said Zayn. "What more could you want?"

"You could easily have stopped Matt. He wouldn't be able to fight someone invisible. Why didn't you?"

Zayn's green eyes bored into mine. "Magic doesn't solve every problem. Why didn't *you* do something?"

"What's the use of feeding and clothing you if you can't even help?" I said, pacing my room.

"I only help those who help themselves," said Zayn, sprawling on the carpet.

I stopped and stared. His words were like arrows in my heart. I'd done nothing to stand up to Matt last year or today. And Matt had grown bolder.

"I freeze when I'm scared," I said softly. "I can't help it." I slumped to the floor and hid my burning face in my hands.

"There's nothing wrong with being scared," said Zayn, sitting down beside me. "Fear is a *good* thing. It keeps you alert and safe in dangerous situations. It's what happens *after* that you have to pay attention to."

"What do you mean?" I asked.

"Imagine what would happen to Matt if I'd helped you. Close your eyes and describe it to me."

I had a clear picture in my head. "He'd be scared because someone invisible had punched him. I would warn him never to touch me or my friend again as he raced away, peeing in his pants." I opened my eyes.

"Violence is never good except when you are protecting yourself," said Zayn. "If Matt tries to hurt you and you defend yourself, he'll get the message. Can you imagine how he would look if you fought back instead of running away?"

"Yes!" I said. "Every detail, down to Matt's frightened expression."

"Good," he replied. "Whenever you're scared, think *really hard* about what you want, and want it *really bad*. Your fear will melt away. *You* should be the one to stop Matt so he never bothers you or Bai again. Not someone he can't see."

"Easy for you to say," I snapped. "Last year Matt shoved my swing so hard, I fell off. I scraped myself badly, even though I'd wished, *really hard*, that I wouldn't fall and get hurt."

Zayn shrugged. "Just giving you pointers. It's up to you to follow them. Or not. I'm on vacation, remember? Ask me for those wishes in a thousand years." He dived into his bed and turned on the TV he'd conjured out of thin air. It even had cable!

I stomped down to the kitchen with the dirty dishes. Zayn was useless except when it came to entertaining himself. Clearly it was going to be up to me to stop Matt.

Chapter Seven

The hands on the clock crawled toward eight forty-five. Bai hadn't come into the classroom. I drummed my fingers on the desk, my eyes glued to the door.

Matt, sitting across the room, glanced at me now and then. He was going to get me after school, and the thought made me want to barf.

Bai and Mr. Walters walked in together as the bell rang. I tried to catch my friend's eye, but he avoided looking at me. When he slipped into an empty seat at the front of the classroom, it felt as if someone had punched me in the gut.

Bai hated front-row seats. Today, it seemed, he hated sitting next to me even more. I could barely pay attention in class. How could I make it up to him? How could I stand up to Matt without freezing or blubbering? At lunchtime Bai disappeared. I didn't see him in the cafeteria or in our special spot in the maple tree. He appeared just as the bell rang at the end of recess. He was mad at me for not keeping my promise, and the only way to make it up to him was to stand up to Matt.

As the clock's hands moved to three fifteen, my stomach shriveled to the size of a pea. It was time to take

Zayn's advice. Except I didn't know if I was brave enough to follow through.

Bai zipped out of class. I ran to catch up with him.

"I'm sorry about yesterday, Bai. I was scared."

He refused to look at me. It was as if *I* were invisible.

I could see Zayn waiting by the school gate. Today he was dressed like a sports coach, with a whistle around his neck and a baseball cap on his head. He fell into step beside me. It didn't make me feel any better.

"Leave me alone, Kiara," Bai snapped after I'd been following him for a few minutes through the park. He was

taking a different route today. "I don't want to be friends with you anymore."

A lump in my throat the size of a tennis ball appeared. I swallowed. Bai had never been this mad at me.

"I mean it, Kiara," said Bai. "Leave me alone, or I'll tell Mr. Walters that you're bothering me."

He sounded serious, his brown eyes hard behind his glasses. I stopped.

"Don't you dare give up, Kiara," said Zayn. "You stay with your friend till he gets home."

"I'm not leaving you alone," I said. "No matter what you say."

"You're too chicken to fight back, so what's the point?" said Bai.

"BOO!" yelled Matt. He'd sneaked up on us while we were arguing.

Bai and I both jumped. Matt guffawed.

"Thank you for running away, Kira-Kira," said Matt. "If you hadn't, I would never have known that your friend is loaded! Now shoo!"

I froze. Matt was right. Because I'd run away, my best friend was his main target now. Bai's face looked gray under his tan, and my chest hurt just looking at him.

"Imagine the outcome," said Zayn, bouncing on the balls of his feet. "You march up to the bully. He's surprised that you're standing up to him. He shoves you, and you punch him in the nose and take back Bai's money. As Matt is running away, peeing his pants, you yell at him never to bully anyone again. Bai is impressed and you are best friends again. Now move! Hup, Two, Three, Four!"

Zayn's voice goaded me on. I unfroze. I lifted one foot, then the other, and marched toward Matt. *I was doing it.*

"You go, girl!" said Zayn, blowing the whistle.

"What are you doing?" said Matt, glaring at me. "Running away is in that direction!" He pushed me hard. I sprawled on the ground as the world spun around me.

Matt had once again emptied Bai's satchel on the ground.

"Money! Now!" said Matt.

"Get lost, bully," said Bai in a quavering voice.

Matt ripped a page from the nearest book he could grab. Bai tried to take it back, but Matt pushed him hard. Bai fell backward and sat there, horrified.

"That's a library book!" said Bai. "Please stop."

Matt ripped out a handful of pages. Bai glanced at me, his eyes wet with tears.

I stood up on shaky legs. *Think of the outcome.*

The only outcome looming in my head was me sitting on the ground next to Bai while Matt tore up my books too. I couldn't do it. My feet turned even as my brain screamed, *No!*

I ran all the way home, the image of Bai's tearful face keeping me company.

Chapter Eight

That night I feigned a stomachache and didn't go down for dinner. Zayn could starve, for all I cared. His stupid advice hadn't worked, nor had he helped.

I was a loser. I'd run away *again*. And because of me, my best friend was Matt's main target. I didn't have the guts to stand up and fight.

I seriously considered telling Mr. Walters everything. Let *him* deal with Matt.

But Matt always caught us while we were in the park, not at school. Could Mr. Walters or the principal do anything about it if the bullying wasn't in school and there were no witnesses?

I *had* to do this by myself. Matt had to know I could stand up to him. It was the only way to stop him and make it up to Bai.

"I'm hungry," said Zayn mournfully. He'd raided my costume closet yet again. Today he was dressed as Pippi Longstocking, complete with red wig and painted-on freckles. If I wasn't so upset, I would have had fun dressing up with him.

"I'm not going down to dinner," I said.

"Go get me something to eat," he said.

I ignored him.

"Please!" said Zayn. "Genies can die of starvation too, you know."

"I only help those who help themselves," I snapped.

"If I start helping myself to food, your mother will notice," said Zayn. "You want that?"

"I'll tell her about you," I said. "No big deal."

"Only you can see me," said Zayn. "She'll think you have an imaginary friend and will schedule a visit with the school psychiatrist."

He had a point. Besides, it wasn't his fault I was a coward.

"I'm feeling better, Mom," I said, shuffling into the kitchen. "May I take a snack up to my room?"

"Of course," said Mom. "You should never go to bed on an empty stomach."

I made six chicken tikka rolls and took them upstairs. A grateful Zayn devoured them all.

"I have a healthy appetite," he said, catching me staring at him. "So what?"

"Whatever," I said and sat down to do some homework. Trying to focus was useless. On every page I could see Bai's scared face, his heaving chest, the ruined library book he would have to replace.

I texted Bai: Sorry. Again. Can we please talk?

No response.

Matt was a vicious bully, but if I could somehow record him in action and threaten to show the video to the principal, maybe he'd stop picking on me and Bai and everyone else. But who would help? None of the other kids in class were friendly enough to help us out. Ever since they had seen Matt picking on us, they'd steered clear, not wanting to risk getting on his radar.

Bai might have helped before, but I was sure now he would never *ever* speak to me again. Matt had cost me my best friend, and I hated him with all my heart.

Zayn dived into his bed and started singing in an off-key voice. I ignored him.

Think! Think! Think! There had to be a way to beat Matt without getting hurt and let him know we were not going to stand for his bullying anymore.

I stared at the beautiful diary Bai had given me a couple of days back. I pulled it to me, wrote my name on the first page and started doodling. I stopped to look up *dealing with a bully* on my computer. All the suggestions involved talking to an adult. Useless, since the bullying was almost always off the school grounds.

Zayn was still singing. He was getting on my nerves.

I'm hot, I'm cool,
too cool for school.
What I touch disappears.
I'm a gen-i-us, my dears!

"Shut up!" I said. "I'm trying to think."

Zayn turned on the TV, still humming under his breath.

First I had to turn Matt's attention back to me, so he'd leave Bai alone.

I'm hot, I'm cool,
too cool for school.
What I touch disappears.
I'm a gen-i-us, my dears!

Zayn sang louder this time. I turned around in my chair and glared at him. He grinned at me. I turned away, thinking hard.

The way I saw it, Matt bullied us only to steal our lunch money. That meant I had to lure him away from Bai and to me by showing him that I had *more* money. And the only way to do that was to break into my puppy fund.

I stared at the picture of the golden retriever pinned to the wall above my desk. My throat closed up, and I blinked back tears. I'd been saving for a puppy for months now and had fifty dollars.

Mom had said if I paid half of the cost, she'd pay the other half.

Bai was more important than a puppy.

I took all the bills out of the box and put them into my backpack. Tomorrow I would make sure Matt picked on *me* by flaunting the money during class.

But what about the day after? And the day after that? Sweat trickled from my armpits. I had just one chance to teach Matt a lesson, and that was tomorrow. What if my courage failed me again, and he made off with all the money?

I'm hot, I'm cool,
too cool for school.
What I touch disappears.
I'm a gen-i-us, my dears!

It seemed like the millionth time that Zayn had sung that stupid stanza, and in the worst voice ever! What did it even mean?

"Wait a minute!" I turned around in my chair to look at him, words tumbling from my mouth as a brain wave hit. I grabbed the notebook on my desk and lobbed it at Zayn. The moment Zayn caught it, it became invisible.

"That's it!" I said, leaping into the air. "That's what you mean by that stupid song. Why didn't you just say so?"

"I'm on vacation...remember?" said Zayn, placing his hands behind his head. "You have to do the work."

"So if I gave you my cell phone to record Matt's bullying, it would disappear when you touched it?"

"Praise be to Allah!" he said. "He has shown the way!"

"I know exactly how to catch that rat tomorrow. Thanks, Zayn."

"Turn off the lights, please," said Zayn. "I need my beauty sleep, and my throat's kinda sore. Didn't think I'd have to sing for so long."

"Serves you right," I muttered.

"I heard that."

Chapter Nine

I couldn't wait to share my plan with Bai. Even though he wouldn't sit next to me in class, maybe I could tell him at recess. After today Matt wouldn't bother anyone again.

Zayn lounged in Bai's seat. He'd woken up and gotten dressed in time to go to school with me, saying he was bored at home. Whatever his reason, I was glad he was here. I needed someone in my corner, even if it was a genie on vacation who had yet to grant me a single wish.

The bell rang. Bai did not come to class. Mr. Walters hurried in and took attendance.

"Excuse me, sir," I said. "Where is Bai Leng?"

"His mother called in to say he's sick," Mr. Walters replied and continued to move down the list of names.

I felt sick too. I figured Bai just didn't want to go through one more day of bullying. What if he decided he never wanted to come back to school? This was all my fault. But I was finally going to do something about it. Today.

I was going to be brave for Bai, for me, and for every student Matt had ever bullied or would try to bully. As we left class during recess, I pretended to stumble and fall when I saw Matt. Money spilled out of my pocket. I gathered up the bills slowly and shoved them into my backpack.

Matt winked at me. *Later*, he mouthed.

"The rat has spied the cheese," said Zayn. He pumped his fist in the air and followed me out to the playground, where he devoured my lunch. I couldn't eat a single bite anyway.

I was grateful for his company even though I couldn't talk to him.

The rest of the day felt as torturous as trying to do math homework with a headache.

"I think I'll get a sick note and go home," I whispered to Zayn late in the afternoon. "I'm not feeling too well."

"You can do this, and I'm with you," he said. "If you run now, I'll sing all night, every night. *Forever*."

"That's blackmail," I whispered.

He gave me an evil grin. "And so much fun!"

I took the usual route home. Before we'd started out, I had handed my cell phone to Zayn and shown him how to record a video.

"Ready?" he said as we got to the deserted stretch of the park where Matt usually showed up.

I walked slowly, my heart pounding, my mouth so dry I couldn't speak. I gave Zayn a thumbs-up sign.

"You can do it," he called out. "For Bai."

"For Bai," I repeated softly.

And there was Matt. Hulking, mean Matt.

"Hand over your money," he said, putting out a grimy palm.

"No! I'm saving up to buy a puppy."

"Woof! Woof!" said Matt. "Don't I make a cute puppy? Looks like you were feeling left out with me picking on Bai. Is that why you brought so much money to school?" He laughed at his joke. "Give it here. Quick."

I saw Bai's scared face in my mind, his eyes pleading for help. Something inside me stiffened. Probably my backbone, which had been missing all this time. My fear melted away and anger charged in, filling me with strength.

"Your bullying ends today," I said. "Go away and we'll forget about this. But if you touch me, you'll regret it."

"Camera rolling," Zayn yelled. "And ACTION!"

I clenched my hands and nodded. "You've bullied Bai and me for too long. It stops now."

Matt laughed. "Acting brave, Kira-Kira? It's a pity that your nerdy friend isn't here to see it."

He pushed me hard. I fell, scraping my face against a tree trunk. Something wet trickled down my cheek.

Ow! And *yes!* I had wanted him to make the first move. Zayn hovered close by, the cell-phone camera aimed at us. It gave me just the boost I needed. I jumped up, drew my foot back and kicked Matt on the shin. He yowled like a mad cat and rubbed his leg. His face was red.

"That was stupid!" he snarled. "I'll teach you a lesson you'll never forget!" He tore my backpack off my shoulders, unzipped it and turned it over. The money fell out. He gathered the bills and stuffed them into his pocket.

Then he grabbed a handful of my
T-shirt and yanked me close. He smelled
of sour sweat and bad breath. He pulled
back his arm. I struggled to get free,

but his grip tightened. I closed my eyes, waiting for his fist to connect with my face. This was going to hurt. I steeled myself.

For Bai. For Bai. For Bai, I chanted in my head.

"OW!" Matt yelped and let go of me.

My eyes snapped open. Zayn was doubled over with laughter.

Matt scrubbed his streaming eyes. "You poked me in the eyes. How did you do it? I didn't even see your hands move."

"Magic!" I replied, winking at Zayn.

Zayn handed me the cell phone quickly. "Playback time."

Thanks! I mouthed.

I waited till Matt opened his watering eyes. I pressed *play* on the video and watched him turn pale. "How, how did you get this? There was no one around us. Who took it?"

"I told you—magic!"

Matt reached out to grab the phone, his face twisted in a sneer. I didn't move. "You can break it, if you like. All my videos and pictures are backed up instantly to the cloud, and I'm getting a new phone soon, so be my guest." I held it out to him with a steady hand, though I knew I would be in loads of trouble if I went home with a broken phone.

"What are you going to do with the video?" Matt asked, his hand dropping to his side.

"Return my money first."

Matt pulled out the bills and threw them at my feet.

"Now get lost. If you ever try to bully someone again, I'm showing this to the principal and our teacher. I might even show it to the whole class."

Matt walked away, his shoulders drooping. I knew this was the last time he'd bully anyone in this school. I had done it.

Zayn and I danced the bhangra. "Ballay, ballay!" we whooped as we circled the tree, even though the cut on my cheek stung and my head throbbed. I wished Bai had been here to join in the celebration.

Chapter Ten

Bai sat in our special spot, munching on a sandwich. When I didn't see him in the cafeteria, I hoped I'd find him here. Though he was still sitting in the front row, I was glad he was at least back at school.

Bai started to pack up as soon as he saw me.

"Please, Bai, watch this, and then you can go."

He took my cell phone and watched the video. His eyes widened when he

reached the part where Matt shoved me into a tree. When the video ended, he handed my phone back to me.

"Who recorded this for you?" he asked.

"A friend who is also sick of Matt's bullying." I remembered Zayn's words. People would think I had lost my mind if I told them about a genie. Plus, I wanted to keep Zayn to myself a little while longer.

Bai shrugged. "Okay."

"I'm really sorry I was a coward. It took me a while to be brave, but I am now. Matt will never bully anyone again," I said. "I made sure of that."

When Bai still didn't say anything, I went on. "I miss my best friend, and I want him back."

"Me too," he said. He scooched over and patted the space beside him.

I climbed up onto the trunk and took out my lunch.

"I have a secret," said Bai. "I only wear clothes made in India. They're the *best*."

I pulled the dragon diary from my bag. "My *favorite* diary is made in China."

"But overall China is still number one," he said.

"You got *that* part wrong, but we'll let it go for today," I replied.

We sat side by side and finished our lunches.

When I went to my room after dinner, Zayn was watching TV.

"Thanks for your help," I said.

"You did the stunts," he said, munching on jalapeño chips. "I was merely the cameraman."

"So, umm, don't you need to go somewhere? Help some other kids in the world?" Since he was on vacation and not granting any wishes, I really didn't need a genie hanging around my room all the time. I could take care of myself now.

"Are you kidding me?" he said. "I've got my own bed to lounge in, a TV *and* a grateful roomie, who loves my singing, to bring me my meals. I'm staying *forever*." He started singing in his off-key voice. "Best friends forever…"

I pulled out my noise-canceling headphones and fitted the large earpads over my head. With a deep sigh, I started on my homework.